JENNIFER NORTHWAY has written and illustrated a number of
acclaimed picture books, including the Lucy and Alice series,
of which *Get Lost, Laura!* (Scholastic)
was shortlisted for the Smarties Award.
In addition to her own work, Jennifer has illustrated books
for many well-known authors, including Jill Paton Walsh,
Floella Benjamin and Mary Hoffman. Her book with
Mary Hoffman, *Nancy No-Size*, (Mammoth) was also
shortlisted for the Smarties Award.
Her work has been televised in England and all over Europe
on children's programmes, and in New Zealand and Australia.

See You Later, Mum!

Jennifer Northway

FRANCES LINCOLN CHILDREN'S BOOKS

This book is for Amy, William, and Mike.
With grateful thanks to Footsteps, The Honey Pot,
and Heather Ridge Infants School
for all their help and support.

On Monday morning William went with Mum
to nursery school for the first time.
He was very excited.

The classroom was full of children. It was very noisy. William stuck close by Mum.

"I'll come back later, shall I?" asked Mum.

"Can you stay?" asked William, feeling shy.

They watched the children painting, but William didn't want to join in.

A little boy was sitting in a big truck in a corner.
He wasn't painting either.

"Did you have fun?" asked Mum on the way home.
"I didn't feel like painting today," said William.

On Tuesday William went with Mum to nursery school.

"Shall I come back later?" asked Mum,
as she hung up his raincoat.

"No, please stay," said William.

So Mum stayed.

The other children were singing songs and clapping. William liked the clapping, but he didn't know all the songs.

The little boy in the red sweater
sat in the big truck and clapped a bit too,
when he saw William clapping.

"Did you enjoy nursery school today?" asked Mum
on the way home.

"Well, I didn't feel like singing today," said William,
"but the clapping was OK. That little boy in the truck
didn't sing either."

On Wednesday morning William and Mum went to nursery school.
The teacher was very pleased to see him.

"Shall I come back later?" asked Mum, as she helped him
off with his boots.

The children were making playdough shapes
and pretend cakes and snakes.
"Can you stay?" asked William.

So Mum sat on a chair. William sat near the other children, and played with some playdough too.

"Do you think that little boy would like some?" he asked Mum.

"He might," said Mum. "Why don't you ask him?"

William went over to the boy and gave him
some of his playdough.

"Thank you," said the little boy, and rolled out
a long snake with it.

"Did you enjoy yourself today?"
asked Mum on the way home.

"I made a good playdough truck," said William,
"and that little boy made a snake. I think he liked me
giving him some of mine."

"I think so too," said Mum.
"Why don't you ask him
what his name is tomorrow?"

On Thursday morning William and Mum
went to nursery school.

William was quite looking forward to it.

"I'll see you later, shall I?" asked Mum,
putting his lunch-box on the shelf.

The children were playing a jumping-up
and falling-down game.

"Please stay," said William. He didn't feel like
jumping up or falling down.

The little boy was sitting in the truck again.
After a bit William went over to him and asked him
what his name was.

"David," said the boy, "what's yours?"

"William," said William. "Can you drive this truck?"

"Only outside," said David, "but it's too rainy
to go out. It has to be a sunny day."

"How was nursery school today?" asked Mum on the way home.

"It was OK," said William. "I've got a friend now. His name is David. He says he can drive that big truck, but only when it's not raining."

On Friday morning William couldn't wait
to get to nursery school. The sun was shining.
When they arrived he took off his coat
and hung it up. He put his lunch-box on the shelf.

David was waiting for William in the truck.
William climbed in.
"Can we go outside today?" he asked the teacher.

She opened the big door, and all the children
pushed the truck into the playground.

"You can go home now, Mum!" called William.
"See you later!"

First published in Great Britain in 2006 by
Frances Lincoln Children's Books, 4 Torriano Mews,
Torriano Avenue, London NW5 2RZ

www.franceslincoln.com

First paperback edition published in Great Britain in 2006

British Library Cataloguing in Publication Data
available on request

ISBN 1-84507-500-5

Printed in Singapore

9 8 7 6 5 4 3 2 1

MORE TITLES FROM
FRANCES LINCOLN CHILDREN'S BOOKS

THE KING WITH HORSE'S EARS
Eric Maddern
Illustrated by Paul Hess

No one knows about King Mark's ears except his barber.
Keeping the secret eventually drives him to the doctor, who advises him
to whisper it to the ground. But sooner or later, the truth will out...

ISBN 0-7112-2079-4

EDDIE'S GARDEN
And How to Make Things Grow
Sarah Garland

What makes Eddie's garden grow? Earth, rain, warm sun,
and all sorts of creatures! Eddie works hard in his garden – digging,
pulling up the weeds and watering his plants. Soon the garden looks wonderful,
full of tasty treats that will make his picnic with Lily, Mum and Grandad
the best one ever! Also packed full of information on how to grow
a garden like Eddie's for yourself.

ISBN 1-84507-089-5

PETS, PETS, PETS!
Kathy Henderson
Illustrated by Chris Fisher

Welcome to the busy, noisy, snoozy, cosy, cuddly, muddly, lazy, dozy,
slimy, grimy, crazy world of Pets, Pets, Pets! This collection of poems
by Kathy Henderson looks at our relationships with our pets,
from the pet shop and the pooper-scooper to the vet and the animal hospital –
not forgetting the magic of babies.

ISBN 1-84507-096-8

Frances Lincoln titles are available from all good bookshops.
You can also buy books and find out more about your favourite titles,
authors and illustrators on our website: www.franceslincoln.com